But It's Just A Game

published by

National Center for Youth Issues
Practical Guidance Resources
Educators Can Trust
ncyi.org

www.ncyi.org

To all of the Jaspers out there! Enjoy. – Julia

Forward By Kim "Tip" Frank, Ed.S., LPC

Author, *Lost and Found: Rescuing Our Children and Youth from Video, Screen, Technology, and Gaming Addiction*

Julia has tackled issues such as handling a parental divorce, bullying, personal safety, grief, and friendship just to mention a few. None of these childhood issues is more important than the one contained in this book. Too many of our young people fall prey to video game addiction. Ninety-seven percent of young people regularly play video games and of these up to fifteen percent become addicted according to the American Medical Association's Council on Science and Public Health. That's over 5 million kids! This book helps parents and professionals "get ahead of the game" by teaching the pitfalls of video game overuse and clearly demonstrating what a healthy balance with video gaming looks like. Imparted in Julia's book are key principles set forth in my latest book, *Lost and Found*, involving prevention of "screen addiction." (See *Tips from Tip* at the end of this book.) Julia does this in a way that is easily understood by kids. By broaching this topic with the young people you know, you will be getting an early start on the preventions of this most recent phenomenon of video gaming addiction.

Duplication and Copyright

National Center for Youth Issues
Practical Guidance Resources Educators Can Trust
ncyi.org

P.O. Box 22185 • Chattanooga, TN 37422-2185
423.899.5714 • 800.477.8277 • fax: 423.899.4547 • www.ncyi.org
ISBN: 978-1-937870-16-4
© 2013 National Center for Youth Issues, Chattanooga, TN • All rights reserved.
Written by: Julia Cook • Illustrations by: Michelle Hazelwood Hyde
Design by: Phillip W. Rodgers • Contributing Editor: Beth Spencer Rabon
Published by National Center for Youth Issues • Softcover
Printed at Starkey Printing • Chattanooga, Tennessee, U.S.A. • August 2013

My name is Jasper, but all of my friends call me "Thumbs" because I'm super-duper good at playing video games. A good gamer has to have really quick thumbs, and my thumbs are SO fast that sometimes I can't even see them move!

With my game controller in my hands,
I'm the boss of my whole world!
I can be who I want and do as I please.
I can get the highest score.

I get all the chances that I need.
If I make a mistake it's ok.
Everyone thinks I'm "it on a stick!"
And the bad stuff all goes away…

Like spelling tests, and cleaning my room,
and my annoying little sister who always
wants me to play house with her…

YUK!

4

"JASPER! GRAB YOUR STUFF AND LET'S GO!

I can hear my mom's voice, but I just can't stop now.
I'm on a new level and I can't figure out how,
to win this part so that I can move on.
I just have to keep playing, but I know that it's wrong!

"Jasper, if we don't leave right now, you'll be late for school!

You're spending way too much time playing that new video game of yours."

Yesterday, I was sitting in math, grading my homework when I heard my teacher say, "As soon as you are finished checking your work, write your score at the top of your paper."

Score??? My score's over ten thousand! Once I get to the next level, I'll have the highest online score ever!

I need to get home and play my new game.
This level is driving me crazy!!!
I think I know what I need to do next.
I just need to stop playing lazy.

Then my head went right into my video game,
and I started my plan of attack.
With my fast thumbs there's no way I can't win.
This I know for a fact!

"JASPER! WHAT ARE YOU DOING WITH OUR TV REMOTE?"

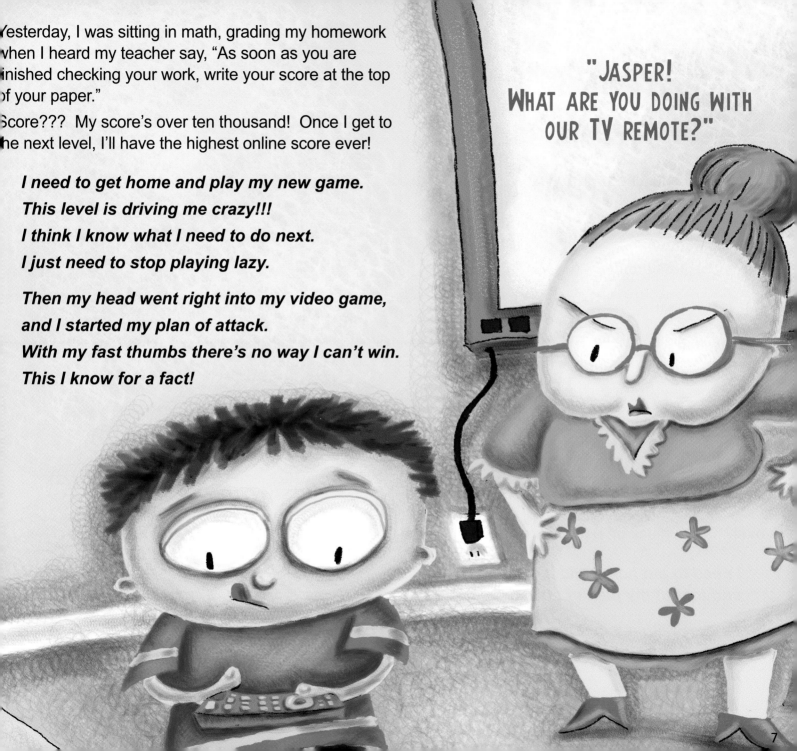

After lunch, Jason Sardoni's uncle came to talk to our class for career day. He's a carpenter, and he brought some of his tools with him and explained how they work.

"This is a miter box. I use it to cut angles.

This is a chalk string. I flip it to make straight lines on wood.

This is a level. I use it to..."

"Level??? I'm stuck on a level, and I need to figure out how to get to the next level.

I need to get home and play my new game, and try out my plan of attack.

With my fast thumbs, there's no way I can't win. This, I know for a fact!"

"Hey Thumbs. What are you doing with my uncle's cell phone?" Jason asked.

"Yeah kid, put that down!"

As soon as I got home from school,
I headed straight for my room.

"Jasper, don't you want your
snack?" my mom asked.

"Not hungry," I said.

*With my game controller
in my hands,*

I'm the boss of my whole world!

*I can be who I want and
do as I please.*

I can get the highest score.

"JASPER,
IT'S TIME
TO GO."

9

I get all the chances that I need. If I make a mistake it's ok.

Everyone thinks I'm "it on a stick!" And the bad stuff all goes away…

Like social studies homework, and practicing the piano, and my annoying little sister who invites me to her tea parties and expects me to show up!

YUK!

"JASPER, GRAB YOUR STUFF AND LET'S GO!"

I can hear my mom's voice, but I just can't stop now.

I'm on a new level and I can't figure out how,

to win this part so that I can move on.

I just have to keep playing, but I know that it's wrong!

"Jasper, we have to leave now or you'll be late for soccer!"

"Can I just stay home tonight Mom? I'm so tired, and I have a ton of homework."

"You love soccer, but if you really do have a lot of homework, I guess you should stay home. Keep in mind though, if you choose to miss practice, you can't play your video game tonight."

"What?"

"Why?"

"Because you have a ton of homework!"

"Never mind, I said. I'll just go to practice."

Soccer practice was kind of a blur,
and my best friend Max wasn't there.

I bet he stayed home to play his game
'cause his mom doesn't care... (I wish my mom was like that!)

I asked my coach to call me "Thumbs."
And then I told him why.

"Fast thumbs won't help you play soccer," he said.
"To get better, you have to TRY!"

As soon as I got home, I got online to see what Max had done.

He'd made it to my level, but I could tell he hadn't won.

"JASPER, PLEASE GET STARTED ON YOUR HOMEWORK, AND WE'RE EATING DINNER AT ABOUT SEVEN."

With my game controller in my hands, I'm the boss of my whole world!

I can be who I want and do as I please. I can get the highest score.

I get all the chances that I need.

If I make a mistake it's ok.

Everyone thinks I'm "it on a stick!"

And the bad stuff all goes away…

Like boring soccer practices, and math story problems, and my annoying little sister who always wants to practice doing hair…ON ME! **YUK!**

I can hear my mom's voice, but I just can't stop now. I'm on a new level and I can't figure out how to win this part so that I can move on. I just have to keep playing, but I know that it's wrong!

"I'm playing my game online against Max, I said. I just about have him beat, and then I'll come down for dinner. GEEZ Mom, what's the big deal? IT'S JUST A GAME."

"Jasper, you're not playing that video game…that video game is playing YOU! LOOK!"

"OH, NO!"

"This gaming thing's making you
act really strange.

You're not the same kid.
You're starting to change.

Your teacher called me,
and she's worried about you.

She says you're getting behind.
Is this true?

You won't eat. You don't sleep.
You won't play outside,

and now this video game
is making you lie.

You're letting a game decide who you are. If you keep this up, you'll never get far."

"JASPER, I LOVE YOU, AND I REALIZE THAT YOU LOVE TO PLAY VIDEO GAMES.

Video games can be a part of your life, but you need to make sure that they don't become your entire life.

"BUT MOM, IT'S JUST A GAME!"

"You're right. That's all it is…a game.

Playing a video game should never be more important to you than spending time with your family, or doing your best in school, or hanging out with your friends."

19

"I understand how you feel Jasper, but I think you need to learn how to switch out this game controller for a **life controller**. To make that happen, we're all going to have to make some changes."

"First of all, we need to move your gaming system out into the family room so that everyone in our family can enjoy playing."

"But mom, we don't have a computer in that room. How am I going to play online with my friends?"

"Well, I think you'll need to quit that for a while. It's really hard to become your own life controller, and playing online with others will make that even harder. Just tell your friends that you need to take a break. I bet you'll be surprised at how understanding they are."

"Next, you'll have to start using your computer for homework only. If you want to download music or play games, you can use the family computer in the kitchen."

"We also need to move your computer out of your bedroom and put it in dad's office." **"WHY?"**

"IT'S REALLY HARD TO BECOME YOUR OWN LIFE CONTROLLER."

"To do it, you'll need to get plenty of sleep, and have a quiet place to study. If your computer is in your room, you might be tempted to let it keep you awake at night."

1 HOUR

"Finally, you'll have to start limiting your fun screen time (playing video games, watching TV, surfing the net) to one hour a day."

"What? That's not enough time! I'll never get to the next level if I can only play for an hour, and my thumbs will get out of shape!"

"You have so many things going on, and to get them all done and do them well, YOU have to be in control of how you spend your time. If you play for more than an hour a day, your game might start playing you again, and your control will be lost. You won't have time for family, you won't have time to do your homework, and you won't have time to hang out with your friends (in person!) Oh, and an hour a day is plenty of time to keep your thumbs in shape!"

The last thing I want is to be out of control, so I listened to what my mom said.

Now at night instead of playing video games, I actually go to bed.

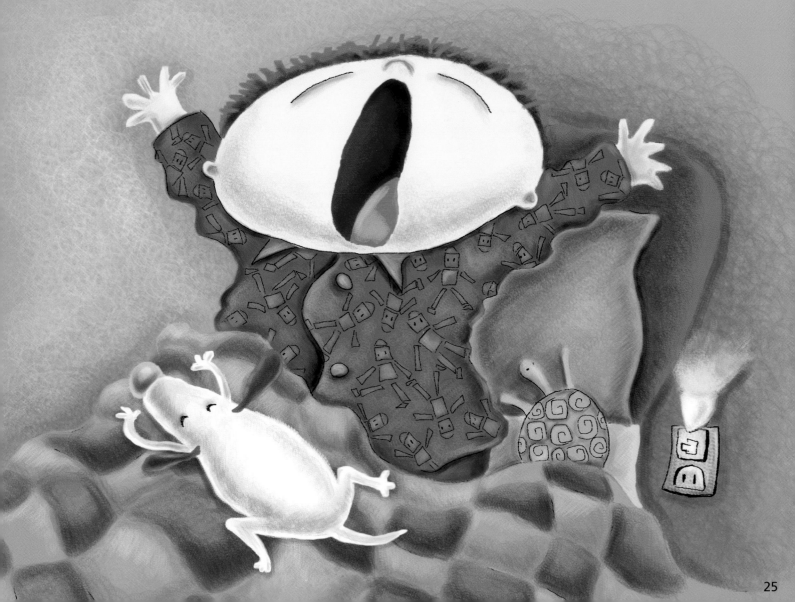

I'M CAUGHT UP IN SCHOOL, MY GRADES ARE GOOD,
AND I'M SPENDING "REAL TIME" WITH MY FRIENDS.

I HAVE A LOT MORE BALANCE NOW,
AND I'M HAPPIER THAN I'VE EVER BEEN!

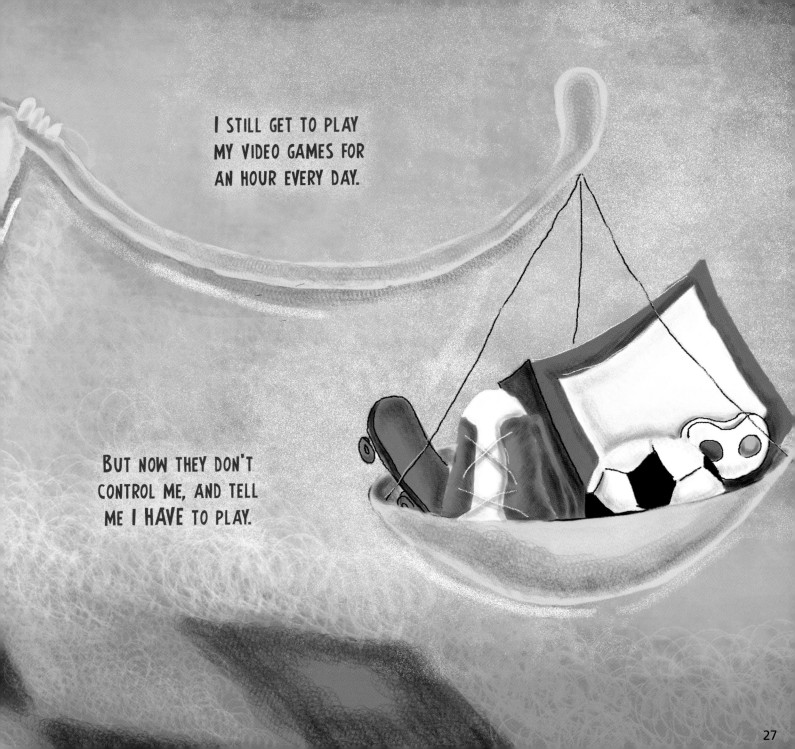

I STILL GET TO PLAY
MY VIDEO GAMES FOR
AN HOUR EVERY DAY.

BUT NOW THEY DON'T
CONTROL ME, AND TELL
ME I HAVE TO PLAY.

I still have the fastest thumbs around;

they're super-duper quick.

And yesterday at soccer,

My coach said I'm "it on a stick!"

When video games took control over me, I had nobody but myself to blame.

But now that I'm my own controller, I can say, "BUT IT'S JUST A GAME."

WHAT PARENTS AND EDUCATORS CAN DO...
(Tips from Tip)

Parental passivity, in many cases, creates an environment of little or no accountability. Taking back the ground, so to speak, toward a healthy relationship with the Internet will involve leading courageously on the part of the parent. The parent or caregiver will need to assertively and lovingly insist on a change of behavior. This starts with the setting of the following boundaries (many of which have been discussed earlier in this book but still apply to initial steps in addressing problematic behavior).

Make sure the rules are reasonable and enforceable.

For example, if a teenager is staying up late and not getting enough sleep, having a technology curfew of 11 p.m. is reasonable versus saying, "No use of technology other than school work will happen in this home." However, if the curfew is not being observed, then privileges are suspended for the next day.

While setting limits, be honest about your concerns.

Let him or her know that there are good reasons for your belief that limits need to be set. The young person can hopefully see that these concerns are legitimate and that the rules are not being made capriciously. Ideally, you and your child or teenager can agree upon the rules.

Insist that non-screen activities occur each day.

Identify activities and hobbies in the home or better yet outside of the home that will bring much needed balance. Activities that involve peers would be best. Setting up a daily schedule can help with this balance. Encourage him or her to take charge of their own schedule but insist on balance with such things as school and home responsibilities along with recreational interests.

Taper "screen time."

While the recommended time limit for Internet use is no more than two hours, it may take a gradual reduction of usage. Step-by-step decreases of screen time toward the two hour limit are at least concrete steps in the right direction.

Limit access to all forms of technology.

If screens are going to be de-emphasized in the home, limit access to the various delivery systems. For example, taking away the gaming console does little good if one has access to games on the computer or Smartphone.

Get family members to commit to backing the parent's decision to set serious limits on technology use.

Ideally, the whole family will "buy into" the importance of not enabling addictive behaviors. Instead a family culture that says that we are all in it together can add support and needed accountability.

If possible, have a separate computer on which to do school work.

As anyone who has ever gone on a diet knows, it is much harder to quit when the object of your addiction is always around you. It is virtually impossible to avoid technology in our society. It is, of course, an integral part of schools today. Having a designated computer for schoolwork only sends a message to the brain that it is time to focus on academics. The recreational uses of technology in its many forms can wait for a designated time as well. This teaches a certain element of self-discipline.

Have a central location for the computer and game console.

This provides accountability and opportunities for families to play together (as opposed to spending countless hours alone in cyber world). At the very least, there are no surprises as to what one is viewing and how long one is on the computer or game console.

Introduce the compulsive Internet user to peers who handle their Internet use sensibly.

Chances are that the Internet addict is only associating with others who are "hooked." Helping him or her to see what a normal relationship to the Internet looks like can be invaluable. The "Ah ha" moment is seeing that most others really can navigate quite nicely to the virtual world and back to the real world.

Support the Internet addict's desire for change if he or she can admit to having a problem.

Parents and various family members' support is much needed. Addictions are not beaten alone. Keep the lines of communication open and a positive relationship going despite the negative attitudes and behaviors of the Internet addict. Tough love is needed, but the tough must not outweigh the unconditional love. *Remember that in the context of a relationship, people are more likely to change.*

Be reasonably patient in the process.

While having reasonably high expectations for improvement, please understand that progress is not always linear. In other words, there will likely be ups and downs and highs and lows. The question is: "Over a period of time, is progress being made?" Young people need adults that believe in them and encourage their progress.

Talk about the underlying issues.

Try to have an honest discussion about whatever issues are happening in the child's or teenager's life. Is there something causing stress? Is there a problem fitting in? Have there been any changes or losses that have occurred? Compulsive Internet use is a sign of deeper problems.

For more information, check out *Lost and Found: Rescuing Our Children and Youth from Video, Screen, Technology, and Gaming Addiction* by Kim "Tip" Frank • Published by National Center for Youth Issues, www.ncyi.org